T0065566

ADULT CHRISTIAN AWAKENING

Anthony "Marsman" Brown

Edited By: Aretha Brown

WESTBOW
P R E S S®
A DIVISION OF THOMAS NELSON
& ZONDERVAN

Scripture taken from the King James Version of the Bible.

WestBow Press books may be ordered through booksellers or by contacting:

WestBow Press
A Division of Thomas Nelson & Zondervan
1663 Liberty Drive
Bloomington, IN 47403
www.westbowpress.com
1 (866) 928-1240

ISBN: 978-1-5127-5776-7 (sc)

Print information available on the last page.

WestBow Press rev. date: 9/30/2016

CONTENTS

STORY 1

VICTORY OVER DEATH

I WAS AT CHURCH service one Sunday morning when I heard the announcement from the pastor urging members to pray for Uncle Louie, my godfather, who was very sick in the hospital. He was my father's best friend and from what I understood from the announcement was that he had cancer and he had a very short time to live. He was eighty-eight years old, the same age my father would be, if he were still alive. He was a very strong Christian. This announcement was a shock because I saw him last week and Uncle Louie was strong and healthy and didn't show any sign of sickness but then again I know that tomorrow is promise to no man so immediately after the Church service I had to go and visit him at the hospital.

Upon my arrival at the hospital I went to Uncle Louie's room and saw him lying on the bed with a broad smile on his face and I asked him, "Uncle Louie how is it I heard you are dying and you're looking so happy and contented?" He replied, "Once you trust and obey Christ Jesus there should be no fear of death because He led the way by conquering death and promised that He had gone to prepare a place for us Christians. And of course you and I know that he is not a liar." I sat in a chair beside his bed and looked at Uncle Louie in amazement and listened how gallantly he spoke with no fear detected in his tone of voice. Uncle Louie went on to say that your body is like a house with the real you on the inside looking out so when your body begins to ache and age, like in his case who had gone way past three scores and ten, the body has to shed and your spirit prepared for your heavenly body. He also went on to say, even if he had the power why should he hold on to a failing body and depend on someone to take care of him when his sight and hearing are failing, there's pain and discomfort in his joints and his memory is lapsing. He said he was not being suicidal it's just the harsh reality of life that everyone have to go through when they begin to age, some will get miserable and get on top of everyone's nerves when they see and feel what age does to their body but it doesn't have to be like that. Christ the great comforter will always be with you and He will never make you bare more than you can take. He also said that if anyone tries to make you feel embarrassed because your body does not function the way it did when you were younger, just smile leave them to time and keep your faith in Christ the Messiah who will guarantee your independence with a new body for your spirit when the time comes.

I listened keenly to the things he had said and I said to him, "Uncle Louie, never before have I heard or read of anyone coming face to face with certain death and sound so convincing, you are one in a million!" Uncle Louie replied, "Listen to me carefully now, **life is temporary,** it's a short journey which you must treasure and serve Christ with all your heart. No one knows the hour so there's no room for error or delay. **Eternity is permanent** whether it's in Heaven or Hell so it will be very important how you live your life if you are going to enter the Kingdom of Heaven to be with Christ. Once you accept Christ as your personal savior and obey Him you will start to focus your mind that the best part of your life is ahead of you. Always remember that if there was no life after death for Christians it means that there is no hope and wickedness is victorious which cannot be the case because **evil cannot defeat Christ**." Uncle Louie went on to say that in the early centuries after Christ's death and resurrection Christians were beaten, stoned and fed to lions before audiences for entertainment and still they grew in numbers, he added that even today in the Middle East Christians heads are chopped off and in spite of all the wickedness demons still quake at the mention of Christ the Messiah name alone. Read (1 Corinthians Ch.15) in the Holy Bible for the full text of the Resurrection of Christ and the dead.

Since we were on the topic of his health I asked Uncle Louie, "Do you have health insurance because this is one of the most expensive hospitals in the US?" He replied, "Don't worry about that, when I was a young cop I remember a conversation I had with an experienced banker at the time who told me that it's not the amount of money you earn it's what you do with it that matters. I took those wise words seriously and carefully invested my money wisely and it's because of the investments that I made why I can enjoy the luxuries here today. Surely when you look at life there were a lot of people that earned far more than I did and can't enjoy this luxury in the end because they did not plan properly for tomorrow."

Uncle Louie went on to tell me a little more of his personal life. He said that he was married once and had one son, unfortunately his wife and son both died in a motor vehicle accident about thirty years ago. He knows that they are now with Christ and as it is now they'll soon be together again. His wife and son were both travelling in a motor car which was hit by a truck driven by a man under the influence of alcohol, the driver of the truck survived and he spent ten years in prison. That driver he said gave his life to Christ and he, Uncle Louie had forgiven him. Uncle Louie also said that he was a vigilant law enforcement officer for forty years. A job he described as not only dangerous but the most difficult because he had to deal mostly with the sins of man. He went on to remind me in the Holy Bible that even God who is so kind, loving and forgiving got frustrated with man when He had to constantly deal with their sins. He said he arrested a number of people for crimes committed put them before the court of law and over ninety percent of them were convicted. He said he had a clear conscience which gave him peace of mind on the job because he did not tell a lie on anyone. Uncle Louie mentioned that he had one concern and it is for the young men of today, who according to the Holy Bible are supposed to be future leaders. He said too many of them are only trying to have a good time and not focusing on their school work. He said they need to be taught from a tender age how Christ worked tirelessly during His lifetime in the flesh doing the work of His Heavenly Father and did not focus on having a good time. Because some young men of today are distracted negatively, their attention is focused in the wrong direction, on drugs, gangs and when they get into fights they depend too much on weapons instead of their fists. He hinted to me the way they dress (sag style) with their underwear on display and the violent disrespectful music they listen to, no decent girl in our days would go anywhere with them. If your father and I were to dress like that when we went to visit our late wives their fathers would chase us away. He went on to say he was not going to lie there and behave as if he was any saint when he was a kid because when he and my father were young they got into fights with other kids too but it was different in those days. They didn't think of using any weapon to hurt anyone and they had manners to the elderly. He said they dressed properly and were far more loving in their thoughts and actions. That's the difference Christ made because they attended Sunday school every week and learned about the teachings of Christ and that is what the kids of today are lacking so he urged me to always remember them in my prayer.

Uncle Louie also pointed out to me that if he could live his life all over again with the same circumstances he would change only one thing. He said that when he retired from law enforcement he turned down a voluntary part time job with an international missionary organization which he regretted until this day. He said that it was the perfect opportunity to spread the gospel of Christ to those in another country who were never exposed to it. A lot of people out there in this world if they had known the teachings of Christ would not have allowed circumstances to bring them to crime when there is hope in Christ. The unfortunate circumstances that have corrupted their minds and brought pain and suffering in their hearts were brought about on them because of the greed of a fortunate few. This he said is sad because when

God created the world there was enough for every human being to live happy all the days of their lives but because of sin a very few have plenty while the majority have nothing. Most people he said who found themselves in grief and suffering did not put themselves there, they were born into it and Christ and no other would have been their only hope for a better life that is why he regretted until this day that he did not accept the offer. Uncle Louie went on to say that the job of a Christian is to win souls for Christ, he won many but could have been more if he had taken up the offer. He was so happy to retire from the stressful job of law enforcement for forty years that all he wanted to do was to finally relax. He said he prayed that God will forgive him.

As I sit there listening to Uncle Louie I remembered when he would hold my hand as a little boy and take me to Sunday school. He was the one who brought me to Christianity and thank God I have not turned back since. Uncle Louie always warned me while growing up that the more technology increases, the more likely man will feel independent and turn away from God hence, I must always be aware of such situations and teach my children the way of Christ and don't depend on anyone to do it for you. He also told me that man is too emotional when it comes to death especially when a Christian dies. Yes, you will be sad and miss the person but on the other hand you have to be glad for them because in his case with all the problems he was facing he had to welcome death as a relief. But if you are a committed Christian it's not good bye when death comes, it's until we meet again on the other side with a re-constructed body which will never ache or age again.

While Uncle Louie was speaking to me he suddenly went silent and had a sign of peace on his face, I thought he fell asleep because the look that he had on his face was the same look a person would have if they had won the Lotto. Uncle Louie was such a confident man that I wasn't sure what was happening to him so I ran out of the room and called the nurse and when they came they asked me to wait outside. About ten minutes after the doctor came out and said that he was dead. I remembered what Uncle Louie said and held my composure by trying not to be sad and just before he died he asked me to read the golden rule of the Holy Bible (Matthew Ch.7 vs 12) at his funeral service, to remind those who attended that it is the only way man can live in peace, (**Do to others as you would want them do to you**).

At his funeral service at the Church there was a large turnout and one thing I will never forget is that my time is going to come one day. At the moment I do not know the day like how Uncle Louie knew his faith was near but from what I have learnt from Uncle Louie I will be prepared to meet Christ, my father and Uncle Louie on the other side. I noticed something that when Uncle Louie's casket was lowered into the grave, a white dove was sitting in the tree top above his grave and when dirt was thrown in the grave to bury the casket the white dove flew away never to be seen again. ONE GOD!

<u>POEM</u>

MANY STORIES WILL BE TOLD

BUT TRUE SALVATION IS FREE AND CAN'T BE SOLD

IN THIS LIFE, MAN IS CALLOUS AND COLD

SO TO PRESS FORWARD YOU HAVE TO BE BOLD

WHY FEAR THE UNKNOWN

WHEN THE WAY OF CHRIST IS KNOWN

DON'T BE DISTRACTED AND WAIT TILL YOU'RE OLD

BECAUSE WHEN IT'S TIME YOU CAN'T PUT DEATH ON HOLD

NOT EVERYTHING THAT GLITTERS WILL BE GOLD

SO BE FAITHFUL TO CHRIST AT ALL TIMES AND A BRIGHT FUTURE WILL UNFOLD

THE END

Story 2

The Man Who Says There's No God

ONCE UPON A time there was a gangster called Boyak who lived during dangerous times in Chicago. Boyak smoked cigarettes, drank a ton of alcohol and was so ruthless that his presence alone drove fear in the hearts of citizens. He trusted no one and lived a life of denial because in his heart he believed there was no God.

Boyak's parents abandoned him on a train line when he was a baby but an elderly woman on her way home from church, luckily found him before the train came along. She had never had any children of her own so she adopted him and named him Boyak after her Russian father. Everything was going well, she used to take him to Church with her and as a very young lad he learned about the Messiah, Christ Jesus. Sadly, one day she became very ill and died when he was just five years old. While on her sick bed, she asked her nephew Carew, who she thought was a nice responsible gentleman, to look after Boyak when she was gone. Unknowing to her, Carew was nothing but a gangster. Her nephew accepted and raised Boyak as his own but Boyak's life took a turn for the worse as he stopped going to Church and started learning the ways of his foster dad. Boyak, while growing up, was expelled from every school he attended and started a life of crime from a very young age because this was all he was exposed to.

When Boyak was in his early twenties he used to sit by himself at the lake and think about the good times he had lived with his adopted mother at home and in Church but he felt so taken over by his luckless circumstances and his fellow men's atrocious lust for evil that he refused to believe there really was a God. Eventually Boyak took over the leadership of his foster dad's gang after Carew was killed by the police while trying to rob a bank. Boyak became so ruthless and notorious that he found himself in and out of jail but, because he had the best lawyers to defend him along with no witnesses daring to turn up, the police were unable to get him convicted in court.

Boyak who was always neatly dressed and had eyes and ears everywhere ruled his cronies with an iron fist, no one dared to disobey his orders. Boyak's strictest rule for his cronies while running his extortion ring was, never kill the goose that lay the golden egg, you just visit them with a baseball and teach them a lesson when they refuse to pay or do not pay on time. It was a very gruesome experience to watch and hear when the people who are referred to as the goose crying out when the bat was used to inflict a stamp of authority on them. It's the only time you would see Boyak smile and no one would dare to snitch.

Boyak found himself as one of the first men in history to be banned by a church because one day while attending the funeral service of one of his cronies called Rahluke, with his usual disrespect for people, places and things he lit a cigarette in church. When reminded by the bishop that the sanctuary was the house of God and could he please extinguish the cigarette, he brandished his Glock pistol and said, "Do you know who I am?!" while walking out. Everyone looked on in silence and the bishop looked at him and said, "May the Lord have mercy on your soul." But what Boyak didn't know is that no one in history had disrespected the Church and escaped God's wrath.

Boyak had one favor he had promised to deliver for Rahluke while he was suffering from gunshot wounds on his hospital bed. The favor was whispered in Boyak ears so that none of the hospital staff who was present on duty could hear. Unfortunately he died immediately after asking the favor. The day after the funeral Boyak went to Rahluke's house and knocked on the door. When the door was opened Rahluke only son named David who is twenty years old opened the door and Boyak said to him politely, "Good evening David, how are you today? Your father died with a broken heart when he didn't see you come to visit him at the hospital, you did not even attend the funeral and you're his only child, that's being ungrateful." "He's a disgrace I hate him and I didn't want to have anything to do with him," David replied. "Oh please come on he had provided for you all these years the things he didn't have when he was young, look at this house you live in!" Boyak said. "I don't care anything about him so don't mention his name to me!" David said. "Well, I'm not going to get into the family business I'm only here to deliver his dying request to you just like he requested," said Boyak. Before David could ask what it was Boyak opened the palm of his right hand and slapped David across the left side of his face sending him flying across the dining table and Boyak said calmly, "Consider your father's dying favor delivered," and walked out.

Being a gangster, Boyak had many enemies. When walking on the streets, always with his gun on his waist, he would constantly be glimpsing back over his shoulders. Unfortunately, one night Boyak was not so lucky as when he was about to enter his vehicle another car with some of his enemies suddenly drove up and opened a barrage of gunfire on him. Although Boyak was hit several times he managed to return the fire with deadly accuracy hitting the driver of the car and caused the car to get out of control and crash in a nearby wall as it sped away. The other occupants of the car weren't lucky because the car exploded. Boyak's cronies heard the gun shots and rushed to check on him. They found him face down on the ground suffering from gunshot wounds but still breathing. His friends rushed him to the hospital where, on arrival, he was taken to the emergency room for immediate operation. But there was an incident that would be remembered by all present while Boyak was being escorted on the stretcher to the emergency room in severe pain in the hospital that night. It was so incredible that even the attending Christian nurse was shocked into speechlessness because she knew Boyak's professed hatred for God and his followers. Boyak's arrival was followed by a sudden and loud thunderstorm. In the midst of the terrifying cracks of thunder from outside and myriad patient's cries inside, there was suddenly a loud shout of **"JESUS, Oh JESUS FORGIVE ME, PLEASE FORGIVE ME"** over and over again, unbelievably coming from Boyak, tears coursing down his face. The nurse could not believe it. But she remembered her pastor's words at church just the morning before saying" Deep in the hearts of men, they know who the Messiah is, but so many choose to live a life of denial and will only acknowledge Him when they are feeling severe pain whether physically or emotionally. She recognized God was doing a mighty work in Boyak's life and, while scrambling along with others to keep him alive, began praying that he might live, and experience the merciful forgiveness of Christ. Boyak recalled later how, while he was on the ground suffering from gunshot wounds he could feel the scorching heat of hades blowing in his direction and at that moment he remembered what he learned in Church as a lad and realized that Jesus was the only one who could save him in that situation before his ghost leaves his body. He also said that when he was at the hospital on what he thought was his deathbed; in the midst of severe pain and agony when he called on the mercy of Christ Jesus the Messiah he suddenly felt a new unexplainable peace that welcomed either death or life.

Boyak miraculously survived an emergency operation and recovered from the jaws of death. After several months with many sessions of physiotherapy and prayer he was fully healed. Boyak became an evangelist, swapped his gun for the Holy Bible praised Christ every chance he got and never returned to the life of a gangster. Boyak gang was eventually dismantled by the police with some of the gang members either dying in shootout with the police or getting a very long prison sentence. Boyak changed his identity and migrated to another country where he lived and died of old age. He led many to Christ and this was his happily ever after. ONE GOD!

POEM

Fools in their heart says there is no God,

And Life itself is just Scientific.

Not so say the wise

Because life with Christ is Fantastic.

If you just humble yourself,

You will find Christ task Specific.

So sincere was Christ, that when He preached and performed miracles,

There was a lot of Traffic.

Serve Christ with all your heart and soul

And His love will be Terrific

Christ brutal death on the cross,

To save us from sin was Horrific.

Don't be fooled because He's kind, loving and forgiving

His wrath can be Catastrophic.

LET'S SHOUT THE MIGHTY NAME OF JESUS, AGAIN, JESUS!
KING OF KINGS, LORD OF LORDS. Amen.

The End

STORY 3

FACING THE CONSEQUENCES

DURING MY LIFETIME I've heard a lot of cold selfish talk about abortion but even though some might not have anything to say about the topic I think that there are two ways to look at it.

The first one is, if two consenting persons willingly get naked and have sweet consenting sex whether unprotected or not and the woman should get pregnant whether accidentally or not then that child has the God given right to be born and there is no doubt about that. Anything to interrupt that birth which was created out of emotional consent is **heartless and wicked!** We have to learn to face the consequences of our actions and deal with it in a humane way. God's word is there in the Holy Bible as a sure guide to everyday living so we should never forget that God says sex must only be done in the context of marriage and stop allowing the devil to use sex to destroy us. We cannot allow below our waist to lead us by not using our brains and then when we get backed up against the ropes we plunge ourselves deeper into a kind of sin that most of our conscience cannot deal with. A lot of women who aborted their first pregnancy were never able to get pregnant again and the doctors who perform these secret abortions and calling them fetus must remember there's a God above who is watching who all of us has to account to one day.

The second one is if a woman is going about her lawful business and is forcibly raped by people possessed by demons, because as far as I am concerned only people who are not in their right mind can do such a brutal act and live with it on their conscience. If during the course of being raped she gets pregnant, that woman has the God given right to determine what she wants to do. No one should condemn her by quoting (Exodus Ch. 20 vs 13) which says, "Thou Shalt Not Kill" or try to make that decision for her by telling her to bare nine months of torture, have the baby and put it up for adoption and in the process making her feel guilty like she did something wrong. She was the one who suffered violation and while some have recovered mentally in a short period of time after the ordeal, others have ended up in a psychiatric ward never to recover. Before anyone start to judge they should read in the same Holy Bible, (Ecclesiastes Ch. 3 vs 3) which says, "There's a time to kill" and (1Samuels Ch. 15 vs 17-19) where God told Saul the king of Israel to, "Go and utterly destroy." Saul was punished because he disobeyed God's command. The same God endorsed the entire Holy Bible so it should always be read in its entirety before quoting verses to make people feel bad. If you want to know how the victim feels you have to first put yourselves in the victim's position, that way you will have an idea of what it's like and have a compassionate mind.

This is the story of a young girl named Bev who was a grade "A" student while attending a prominent high school in New Jersey where she was born and raised. Not only was she a top student she also won a scholarship to attend a prestigious university in the coming months. That dream was almost never materialized. After her High School graduation ceremony she attended a party held by her graduating class and a lot of wild things took place. Bev disobeyed her parents and had a drink too many then had several dances with her high school crush from the 7ᵗʰ grade, Troy. After they finished dancing they left the party and had unfortunate unprotected sex in the back seat of his car. It didn't end there because a few weeks after the party, she missed her period. When she went to the doctor to get tested it came out positive for pregnancy.

When she went to Troy's home and told him about the test he asked, "How am I sure that the baby is mine? I think it's best if you get rid of it." She said, "Are you crazy, even though I was disobedient to the scriptures I still pray and ask Christ Jesus for forgiveness. I know this might set me back in life but I am not going to be a part of any wickedness. From my understanding of the Holy Bible **people kill because of fights** not because of love which I thought we had." He hissed his teeth, slammed the door in her face and walked away. Bev went home and sat in her room and cried bitterly, trying to find a way to tell her parents who were devoted Christians and had high expectations for her. She knew she couldn't keep it for long because it would soon begin to show so the next day she told her parents she wanted to speak to them. When she sat down with them her father jokingly asked, "Don't tell us that you want a raise in your allowance already and you haven't gone to college as yet" Bev said, "It's not that I want to speak to you about, I went to the doctor and did some test the other day and it came back positive." "What test?" asked her mother in a very serious tone of voice. Bev said without any more hesitation, "I'm pregnant, I'm sorry I didn't mean for it to happen, I got carried away at the graduation party and now I don't know what to do." When her mother heard she fainted and her father said, "Look what you did now I have two sick persons on my hands, by the way who is the father?" Bev told him that Troy is the father but he is denying it and told her that she should get rid of it.

When Bev's father went to see Troy's father it got even more frustrating because Troy's father told Bev father that they should get rid of it and there's no way he is going to allow his unemployed son to be fathering any child at eighteen years old. Bev's father left the house feeling very disappointed at what he heard and started to feel so depressed that he took a week off from his work in order to get his mind together.

When Bev father got home and saw her he said, "One thing I know for certain, I am not going to serve two masters and be a part of any wickedness. Why are you children so disobedient! What about what you heard in Church of no sex before marriage because now your university scholarship will surely go up in flames!" Bev started to cry and ran to her room, her mother warned him, "Take it easy honey before you start getting sick too, the damage is already done."

After several weeks had passed and the pregnancy was now starting to show, many relatives who knew Bev's potential in school was still telling her that she should get rid of it before it's too late but Bev simply refused to do it because she did not want the wrath of God to go against her.

One day when Bev pregnancy had reached an advanced stage she went to see Troy and when she saw him she said, "You haven't come to see me once and offer some form of support with all the disappointment that I am facing." He said, "What should I do I told you to get rid of it and you refused, well too bad I am not working and I'm advising you and that thing in your belly that you claim is mine not to come back here because you're not welcomed." Bev replied, "Be a man and get a job because I can't work in this condition! I can't allow my parents to be carrying the financial burden alone. You're going to tell me that not even baby powder you are going to buy when the time comes?" "Use ashes!" he said. That statement made Bev finally wake up to the harsh reality that she fell in love with someone who couldn't care less about her existence and went straight back to her house never to visit him again.

About ten rocky years had passed and Bev with all the disappointed she faced during her pregnancy managed to have a handsome son named Timothy who took after her footsteps and was very bright in school. Despite her setbacks and being a single parent she continued to attend Church with her son and begged God for forgiveness. She also managed in spite of everything to attend university and majored in her required discipline. Thanks to God and her forgiving parents who did not give up on her and this gave her a top job in Manhattan. As for Troy he never studied further than high school and never came to see Timothy once, all his attention was focused on the horse race track which he attended daily and ended up becoming a gambling addict.

Ten more years had passed, making Timothy almost twenty years old. He had received a track and field scholarship to a prestigious university and started preparing himself to represent the US at the Olympic Games that summer. That year something happened that if I was ever doubtful I would now be sure that there is a great God in Heaven named Christ Jesus. A friend of Bev who knew about what took place during the pregnancy visited the race track and heard Troy telling some people that Timothy who had become famous is his son when he heard him winning medals after medals. He was also bragging how he took care of him from he was a baby and how much Timothy resembles his mother the most. This is a situation that Christians have to face that no matter what was done against you, you cannot retaliate but just turn the other cheek and forgive. Bev had forgiven and forgotten about Troy a long time ago but if he is ever going to have any peace of mind The Holy Bible which is God's word says he'll have to repent and come to Christ Jesus. ONE GOD!

<u>POEM</u>

WHEN GOD SAYS HE'LL TAKE CARE OF YOU

THAT'S EXACTLY WHAT HE'LL DO

HE'LL BRING PEACE AND LOVE AT YOUR DOOR STEPS

LIKE A DREAM COME THROUGH

YOUR BLESSINGS WILL MULTIPLY

AND YOUR ENEMIES WILL BE FEW

IN CHRIST, THERE'S ONE GOD

SO DON'T BE FOOLED BY ANY OTHER VIEW

JUST KEEP THE FAITH AND FOCUS

BECAUSE HE WILL NOT MAKE YOU SWALLOW MORE THAN YOU CAN CHEW

THE END

STORY 4

WHAT YOU CAN ACCOMPLISH WITH CHRIST

S OME YEARS AGO there was a sweet, God faring lady named Lois who worked at a factory in Detroit. She was loved and respected by everyone who lived in the district where she lived and likewise it was the same situation at work. She always had a smiling face and was so content with serving Christ Jesus that she didn't allow anything to worry her and everywhere she went she represented Christ well.

Lois also loved and took a lot of pride in her work. She was never absent from work; late or resentful to her supervisor in whatever task she was given to do. She was the first to arrive at work in the mornings and the last to leave in the evenings after work.

One day Mr. Martin, the chairman of the company she works for, started to notice and admire her dedication to her job. Where his office is located he can see every worker who comes in or out of the premises. What he admired most about her was that she was always smiling and not looking grumpy like the other workers, who were always complaining about low wages and not enough benefits. One afternoon he invited Lois to his office to have a talk with her because he wanted to know what were the motivating factors behind her unusual contentment, none of the supervisors have ever complained about her. When Lois came to his office the chairman introduced himself and noticed that she still had that pleasant, confident smile and not showing any signs of nervousness that the other workers would show when they are called to his office. Mr. Martin asked, "What is making you so humble, so contented and so dedicated when you are not given any preferential treatment over the other members of staff who show nothing but grumpiness?" She answered, "I serve a God name Christ Jesus who assured me in the Holy Bible that I must not worry and He will take good care of me no matter what situation I am in. He is my provider, not man, sir." The chairman said, "I am commending you on your good work attitude and this meeting has opened my eyes on a number of things. Thank you Miss Lois you can go back to work." "I am grateful to have spoken with you sir," said Lois.

The meeting with Lois and Mr. Martin did not go down well with the other supervisors because he started to talk highly of Lois and this made the supervisors jealous of her. One day Lois was reading her Bible and praying during her break time and one of the supervisors who is an atheist, saw her and wrote a report to the chairman saying that Lois was causing religious problems at work in the name of her God. Mr. Martin read the report and asked to see both of them in his office the next morning. When the supervisor who wrote the report and Lois met with Mr. Martin in his office the next morning, the supervisor presented his case against Lois to him.

Mr. Martin listened tentatively and replied to the supervisor when he was finished presenting his case. Mr. Martin said, "You have brought several members of staff before me for disciplinary action and this one is the most outrageous. I have read your records here in your file and I've seen where not only have you been making unfair complains against workers but they have also been making complaints against you. You were late on several occasions and was even caught sleeping on the job once. What you don't understand is that the company rules are for every worker including supervisors. You seem to be a person who will always see the speck in other workers eyes and not see the plank in yours. What you claim Lois did was done during her break so the case is dismissed." Before Lois left the office she asked Mr. Martin, "Sir, where did you get that phrase about speck in eyes and remove the plank from your eyes?" Mr. Martin replied, "Ever since our last meeting I started reading the Holy Bible and loved the teachings of Christ Jesus so much that I accepted Him as my personal savior, thanks to you of course." "Praise the Lord!" said Lois.

The following week there was a big shake up at the work place, Lois was promoted to supervisor and everyone was given a raise of salary and lived happily ever after. ONE GOD!

POEM

WHILE EVERYONE WAS IN THEIR ZONE

CHRIST CALLED ME ON THE PHONE

HE PROMISED NEVER TO LEAVE ME ALONE

WHILE HE PREPARED MY HEAVENLY HOME

HE SAYS NO ONE CAN CAST ANY STONES

BECAUSE WE'RE ALL SINFULLY PRONE

NO MATTER HOW YOU THINK YOU'VE GROWN

THIS WORLD WILL ONLY MAKE YOU MOAN

HE WARNED THAT TRICKSTERS WILL COME IN HIS NAME

BUT HE WILL ALWAYS BE THE SAME

THE END

STORY 5

MONEY CAN'T REPLACE CHRIST HAPPINESS

NOT LONG AGO there was a poor man called Korey, who lived in a district named Blue Hill. Everyone in the district was related in some way or the other but apart from that they were kind loving people who looked out for each other. They survived off the land and made good use of the little they had. When the pressure of life took its toll on them, some would speak openly about going to the big city to work and try to get rich. But not everything that glitters is gold because people who lived and worked in the big city had a different frame of mind, they wanted to one day come to the country to get away from the hustle and bustle of the polluted city life. The country life might be slower but history has shown us that living in the country is healthier and you will live longer hence more contentment.

One day Korey, who is also a gambler, went and bought his regular purchase of lotto tickets and after years of purchasing he finally won a $20,000,000.00 first prize.

This made him very happy and made him think that he can finally say goodbye to poverty. What he didn't understand was that everyone in the district who was not so bright was also celebrating and thinking that they can also say goodbye to poverty for good.

A few days before he would collect his money most of the people in the district would come to him and tell him how much they want out of the winnings, what they were going to do and how big the celebration should be. Korey started to ask himself, "This money belongs to me, I'm the one who won it so why are all these people making all these demands? And when all the demand is totaled it's going to come to more than the winnings itself?" So Korey made a list of all the people and how much they are going to get and pinned it on a tree where everyone could see it. This didn't go down well with some of the people on the list because they were expecting a lot more and the ones who weren't on the list started making serious threats. All of a sudden a shadow of doom started to cover the district and the people who lived caring and loving with each other for years started to allow greed, selfishness and hate to wipe out decades of Christ like living. Everyone would lock themselves in their homes not speaking to each other, the streets at night especially would look like a ghost town and Korey the lotto winner had to watch his back and try to sleep with one eye open. Things have gotten so bad that Korey had started to think that winning the money was a curse because before, everyone was rich in spirit and contented with the little they had.

On the day of prize collection in the city, Korey went and collected his prize and faced his first disappointment because when tax was deducted almost half the money was gone. When Korey returned to the district with his money he saw some of the buildings destroyed and the people standing in the open because there was a tornado while he was in the city. This was the first time any disaster like this has ever happened in the district – it was as if God had punished the people for sinful behavior. Things weren't looking good so Korey called a meeting which everyone attended. Everybody looked into themselves and realized that before the lotto prize money Christ Jesus the only true and living God was present with them and they started to feel ashamed because of how they had behaved. A night of prayer and fasting was held and after the meeting they all realized that no money can take the place of Christ like living and begged God for forgiveness. The district was unified once again, the streets were lively with people and the lotto prize money was used to fix the buildings in the district that was destroyed hence, they lived happily ever after. ONE GOD!

POEM

FORGIVE US LORD, FOR GOING BLIND

BUT YOUR WORD HAVE MADE US SEE

TO BE SUBJECTED TO THEE

IS HOW WE SHOULD BE

OUR FAITH WAS TESTED

AND WE FAILED YOU LIKE THE FIG TREE

TRUSTING IN YOU O'LORD

WILL ALWAYS SET OUR CONSCIENCE FREE

AND GRACE AND SALVATION IS THERE FOR US

WITHOUT EVER PAYING A FEE

THE END

STORY 6

BE CAREFUL OF WHAT YOU WISH FOR

ONCE THERE WAS a decent young Christian gentleman named Jerome. He lived with his wife and two children in the city of Atlanta. He worked as a janitor in an office complex and was the lone bread winner in his family. Jerome's life was from paycheck to paycheck and he was unable to save anything for a rainy day. This made his family life very fragile because his greedy wife would nag him constantly. Jerome constantly tried to find a better job but the job market was very scarce and whenever anything came up on the market, you would have to know someone influential to speak on your behalf. The nagging from Jerome's wife had gotten so bad that it frustrated him to the extent that he didn't even want to go home after work.

One night after Jerome finished having his nightly devotion, his wife started nagging him again and it started an argument between them. This made him so angry that he turned to the Lord in prayer and said, "How much more should I take Lord, I wish that this woman be out of my sight!" Jerome kissed his children good night and retired to bed not remembering what God said about letting the sun go down on your anger (Eph. 4:26).

The next morning when Jerome woke up, his wife was still unusually asleep because she was always the first to get up in the mornings. He got up and went to the bathroom without saying a word. When he came out of the bathroom she was still sleeping so he went to the kitchen and prepared his breakfast, ate, kissed his children and was about to leave for work when he turned around to kiss his wife when he noticed she was not moving. Jerome touched her and said, "Honey I am leaving now." He noticed she did not answer so he touched her again and said, "You got to get up now and monitor the children I'm running late." She still didn't move so he shook her harder and she still didn't respond so he went to the telephone and called the ambulance service. When the ambulance crew arrived they put her on a stretcher and put her in the back of the ambulance and sped away to the hospital. Jerome could not go with them and leave the children alone so he got them dressed and called work to tell them that he would be unable to make it. They all proceeded to take the public transportation to the hospital. All this time no one knew what was happening to her because she did not complain about any sickness.

When Jerome and the children three and five years old arrived at the hospital and made enquiries about his wife he was told that she had fallen into a coma and the doctors could not find the reason for it. No one knew how long this would last and Jerome started to worry because he had to go to work and someone had to take care of the children so he called his aunt and asked her for assistance with the children and this she did.

One month passed and his wife was still in a coma. Life became even more unbearable for Jerome because he started blaming himself for asking God to take her out of his sight. One night he went by her hospital bed side with his Holy Bible and a little poem he wrote for her because it was Valentine's Day. The doctor also assured him that she can hear whatever he says but she will not be able to respond.

POEM

HOW EXTRAODINARY IT IS

WHEN THE SKY MEETS THE DEEP BLUE SEA

HOW AWESOME IT IS

WHEN THE SUN RISES IN THE MORNINGS AND SETS IN THE EVENINGS

HOW PHOTOGENIC IT IS

WHEN THE MOON SHINES AND LIGHTS UP THE LONELY NIGHT

HOW ROMANTIC IT IS

WHEN THE STARS SPARKLE IN YOUR EYES SO BRIGHT

HOW COLORFUL IT IS

WHEN ROSES BLOOM IN THE SPRING AND THE BIRDS BEGIN TO SING

THEN, ON THIS VALENTINE'S DAY

LET'S REFLECT ON THE MOMENTS WE SHARE

TO BE ONE WE WILL CHERISH SO DEAR.

When he finished reading the poem he started to pray in earnest because one thing he knew for certain when all men have failed the great Christ Jesus will never fail. Jerome prayed and prayed for hours and suddenly he saw when his wife made a little twitch and moved her head. He ran out of the room and called the nurse, immediately the doctors took over and asked Jerome to leave the room. After about an hour the doctor came out and told Jerome that she is fine and he could now go in and see her. But before he went in the room one of the doctors asked him, "What did you do in there because we almost gave up hope?" Jerome replied, "All I did was to have faith in Christ Jesus the greatest healer."

Jerome took his wife home the next day and she was more understanding never to nag him again. ONE GOD!

THE END

Story 7

Honor Your Parents

ONCE UPON A time there was a man named Ralph who was thoughtless and selfish. He lived with his wife, two children and his mother who was old and God fearing in a small family house at the edge of a town called Brimstone.

Ralph's two children were growing up and the space in the house was getting smaller so he had a discussion with his wife about creating more space for the family to live comfortably. Ralph said to her, "Honey, I'm going to take my mother to the old age home to stay so we can have more space in the house" His wife looked at him in surprise and said, "Are you crazy? She has been like a mother to me, how could we do such a wicked act, what are we going to tell the children?" Ralph replied, "Don't worry I will tell them that she has gone to live at Disney Land and you know how they love Disney Land" His wife replied, "They are going to grow up and one day know the truth. Please leave me out of this. You are going to be sorry!" No matter what Ralph's wife said, he was determined to carry out his heartless plan for, as the head of the family, his decision was final.

The following day, Ralph took his mother to the old age home to live among strangers and left her there with a broken heart. Before he left her she gave him a letter in a sealed envelope and told him not to open and read until he arrived home. Ralph left without so much as a look back, because in his heart his mother was old, her time had expired and she could die at any moment. Faith was on Ralph's mother side because, being a strong Christian, though staying at a strange place away from family, she was always comforted by angels while she prayed and read the Holy Bible.

When Ralph arrived home he did what his mother told him to do and opened the envelope. In it was a little poem she wrote on a piece of paper the night before she left the house. It read.

POEM

WHEN YOU'RE SAD AND LONELY

TIME WILL TRAVEL SO SLOWLY

WHEN YOU'RE JOYFUL AND HAPPY

TIME WILL TRAVEL MORE QUICKLY

CHRIST IS MY MASTER

SO I WILL FEAR NO DISASTER!

SERVING HIM IS MOST DIVINE

SO I WILL NEVER WORRY ABOUT THE HANDS OF TIME

WHILE YOU WILL BE HAVING A GOOD TIME

CHRIST WILL COMFORT AND MAKE ME FINE

THE WORDS OF CHRIST WILL ALWAYS SHINE

SO NO ONE CAN STOP THE HANDS OF TIME

MAY GOD FORGIVE YOU MY SON!

During the weeks after taking his mother to the old age home Ralph found that all his friends in the neighborhood had withdrawn from him because of his treatment of his mother. They all expressed sadly how such a wonderful lady could end up in such a situation. Although estranged from his friends, Ralph found that to be minor because his greatest enemy was now his conscience. Ralph would sit by himself from time to time and be pursued by memories of the love and kindness that his mother had shown him while growing up. But it still did not change anything as he was so blinded by sin that he still played tough.

One day while Ralph was sitting in his living room his son Craig came and sat down beside him. "Daddy we have not seen grandma in nearly a year, is she having such a good time that she has forgotten and not called us?" Craig asked still unaware that his father had been lying all this time about his grandmother being at Disneyland. His father replied, "She is fine son." Craig looked at him and said, "When I grow up, and you get old like grandma, I'm going to take you to Disneyland where you can have lots of fun too daddy." Ralph jumped up out of his chair in a state of shock and said to his wife who was standing nearby hearing the conversation, "You see how ungrateful children are!" Ralph's wife laughed loudly and said, "What comes around goes around, you think God would make the wickedness that you have done to your mother go just like that. You need to repent and change your ways!"

Ralph finally came to his senses and realized what was hanging over his head, knowing his children could easily take him to any old age home when he was old. Ralph jumped in his car the next morning, drove several miles to the old age home and brought his mother home where she belonged. Ralph's whole attitude changed, he was more loving and understanding with his family and even began attending Church where he started serving the Lord Jesus Christ. Ralph regained the forgiveness and respect of all his friends and relatives and he lived happily ever after. ONE GOD

THE END

STORY 8

ONLY CHRIST WAY WORKS

BRUCE, NOW AN adult is a recovering drug addict who had to attend a substance abuse class every Thursday as part of his therapy. About ten people on average attend this class and the age varied from late teens up. All were former abusers of various drugs that included alcohol, cocaine and opium etc. Only one female was in the class, an eighteen-year-old girl who showed great potential at school and found herself addicted to cocaine and pregnant. Although everyone in the class was from differing backgrounds they all shared one thing in common, they all stubbornly did things their way and not Christ Jesus way. They all paid a serious price for their disobedience to the scriptures. Sometimes Bruce would go by the lake and sit by himself remembering the good times he had with his dad and asked himself what was he thinking and why did he chose the type of friends that he had. He just didn't need them and he was not going to blame them for his condition because when he travelled around the country he saw billboards telling him to leave drugs alone. He saw advertisement on television, he heard it on the radio, he heard it in school and church and what's worse he saw with his own eyes people that drugs destroyed and he still took it so he can only blame himself. Christ Jesus had given him a second chance to put things right so he will not fall prey to the devil again. Bruce grew up in Dallas, Texas in a middleclass family and attended the best schools in Texas. He had good respectable friends at Church but he always saw their disciplined way of life as boring. His parents were warm loving Christians who worked very hard to give him everything he ever wanted but because he let down the high expectations they had for him, he was so ashamed that he didn't miss any of the substance abuse classes.

It all started when Bruce was about fourteen years old, hanging out with some of his classmates who were not from a Christian background. His friends smoked cigarettes and because Bruce wanted to be seen as cool he would hang out with them wearing his pants below his waist (sag style) and took part in the smoking of cigarettes. This went on for about two years, this means he was now sixteen year old and finding cigarettes getting too light so he started experimenting on something heavier so they switched from cigarettes to ganja.

This was where the real problems started. Bruce's grades in school began to drop and his parents started to get on his case but he had to have his own stubborn way. He continued smoking ganja for about two more years undetected until one day at a spring break party he tried some heavier stuff; cocaine. A few days after the spring break party Bruce developed a desperate crave for cocaine which started to drive him insane, the real addiction now stepped in because Bruce wanted it more and more and more, which made him a junkie for hard drugs.

One day Bruce parents started finding out that things were going missing in and around the house, including cash from his mother's handbag. When Bruce was confronted he denied everything so his parents set up a secret camera in the house when Bruce was not at home. A few days after Bruce father missed a hundred dollar bill from his wallet. He confronted Bruce saying, "Did you take any money from my wallet?" Bruce replied, "No daddy!" So Bruce's father decided to check the secret camera that Bruce didn't know about in in his presence. To Bruce's surprise when they all viewed the monitor, Bruce could be seen crawling on his belly when his parents were sleeping in the bedroom and taking the money. Bruce is now cornered and speechless and could not deny anything this time. His embarrassing addiction caused a lot of pain at home because his father fired two helpers because of the ongoing disappearance of items which included money. "Why are you doing all this, I gave you everything you ever asked for?" asked Bruce's father. When Bruce started to confess, his mother broke down in tears when she heard about the cocaine. "You need professional help, I am taking you to see a Christian psychiatrist because medicine alone is not going to solve your problem!" said Bruce father.

The next morning Bruce was taken to one of the best substance abuse recovery home in Dallas, the Church that his parents attended would pray for him. The members along with his parents would visit him from time to time to monitor his recovery. It did go well and Christ Jesus was a very important part of the recovery because only He, Christ Jesus could reach that inner part of his heart which doctors cannot reach to stop the dangerous addiction from flaring up again. ONE GOD!

<u>POEM</u>

WHAT WAS I THINKING

WHILE MY WHOLE LIFE WAS SINKING

TIME SPENT WITH MISGUIDED FRIENDS

WAS PART OF A STUPID TREND

I ALLOWED SUBSTANCE TO CONTROL MY MIND

AND TRY AS I MAY I COULDN'T UNWIND

MY LIFE BECAME A ROLLER COASTER RIDE

BECAUSE I DIDN'T LET CHRIST CHOSE THE TIDE

OH LORD, IT WAS A DANGEROUS GAME

AND I HAVE MYSELF TO BLAME

THANK YOU CHRIST JESUS FOR FORGIVING ME!

THE END

STORY 9

TRUST AND OBEY CHRIST

EVERY EVENING, MONDAY to Friday after leaving work about 5 o'clock I would drive the same route on the way home. This route would take me on a particular road where there is a park that people would go and jog or sit and meditate. While going past the park I would slow down and observe what is taking place and there is one particular incident that was brought to my attention. There was this young man looking to be in his mid-twenties on his knees at the same spot praying every day. So after about five months of seeing this I decided to stop one evening, take a seat in the park to see how long he would pray for. To my surprise this prayer lasted for approximately one hour and when he was finished he got up and left.

One Saturday evening I was on my way to the supermarket, I decided to drive past the park to see if the young man would be there and to my surprise he was at the same location at the same time. I stopped and had a seat in the park beside where he was praying because this time I decided that I had to have a word with him so I waited until he was finished. When he got up and was brushing off his knees to leave I said to him for the first time, "Young man, my name is Matthew what's yours?" He looked at me and said, "Stephen." I told him that I was also a Christian and I was a regular visitor to the park and seen where he had come and prayed at the same location every day. Stephen replied, "Yes, this is my way for giving God thanks for the enormous talent that He had bestowed on me despite my problems." When Stephen said that he stretched out his arms and showed me his deformity, one arm was longer than the other that I hadn't notice until he showed me.

We became good friends and the following Saturday we met again at the same location and he opened up more and started telling me about his life. Stephen told me that he was in this deformed state because his mother who people say was a prostitute, smoked and drank a lot of alcohol during pregnancy. Sadly, she died when she was giving birth to him and he was raised by his grandfather ever since because he had known no father. Stephen said his grandfather was an atheist but saw to it that he attended school regularly.

Stephen told me that while attending school he faced some major obstacles. He was teased and called names like "cripple" because of his deformity, bullied by the bigger boys and constantly told that he can't do this and he can't do that, and that he would never be good enough. Stephen told me that he loved playing table tennis but because of the constant taunting by the students it started to rest on his mind and he started believing that they were true, many a times he said he broke down in tears.

One Sunday he was watching a Christian Evangelist on television and heard some quotations which were read from the Holy Bible. (**In Matthew Ch.19 vs 26 Christ Jesus said, "For man it is impossible but for God all things are possible."**) (**In Matthew Ch.17 vs 20 Christ Jesus said, "If you have faith the size of a mustard seed, you will say to this mountain, move from here to there and it will move and nothing will be impossible to you."**) (**Philippians Ch. 4 vs 13 stated that, I can do all things through Him (Christ Jesus) who strengthens me.**) This energized Stephen this made him want to know the God of the Holy Bible so he started saving his lunch money which he used to buy a copy of the Holy Bible. Stephen said he started reading the Holy Bible in earnest and he learned more and more to believe in Christ the Messiah. He started coming by the park to pray every day for the past ten years.

Stephen told me that although people used to laugh when he serviced the ball in a table tennis game because of his deformity, he developed so much internal strength when reading the Holy Bible that his table tennis skills improved tremendously. He started winning tournaments after tournaments and was just recently beaten by the US champion in the all States final. Everyone started to praise and admire him, a tremendous turnaround from the taunting he used to receive when they saw his courage but Stephen said that all praises should really go to the Messiah Christ Jesus who inspired him with His teachings in the Holy Bible.

Stephen and I became best friends and he started attending the same Church that I attend. Stephen will be getting married soon to my cousin and I will be the best man. ONE GOD!

<u>POEM</u>

HOW CAN MAN REJECT

WHO CHRIST DID NOT EJECT

NONE IS PERFECT

SO WHY LET ANOTHER FEEL IMPERFECT

THE ONLY SURE LOVE

IS WHEN CHRIST IS PROJECTED

WHATEVER CHRIST SAYS

IT MUST BE ACCEPTED

BECAUSE WHEN YOU COME IN CONTACT WITH HIM

YOUR SOUL IS PROTECTED

THE END

STORY 10

THE WHITE COLLAR CRIMINAL

MY NAME IS Prince King, my friends call me Mr. Smart and I was recently convicted by a court of law, to twenty five years in prison for fraud. When I first came through the prison gate and heard the loud sound it made when it shut behind me every nerve in my body shook, this is when I woke up to the harsh reality and immediately started to make adjustment to a long life behind bars. People don't willingly come to a place like this so I am writing this letter from my prison cell and I would like every young person especially to read it so they will never make the same mistakes that I made. I went from a king to a jack in a short space of time so I'm asking you please trust in Christ Jesus because it doesn't make any sense trying to gain the world and lose your freedom/soul in return. When I was on the streets I was a ladies man and as you know there are no ladies inside here so you have to hold the strain and develop strong mind control in order to remain straight. On the streets I gave orders, in here I take orders from the prison wardens and when they say jump the only question you can ask is, "How high?" You cannot survive as a loner inside here, If you weren't a member of a gang on the streets you have to join one inside here or risk the chance of being gang raped, someone has to watch your back especially when you are taking a bath. One thing I learn since being here is that you must reject all voluntary favors to you by other prisoners because if you accept they are going to behave as if you owe them and one day ask you for one which you won't be up to.

It all began in Miami, Florida where I grew up in a small middle class family of four; my father, mother, sister and myself. I was the younger of the two and the one who was spoiled and wouldn't satisfy. I did extremely well in schools and I graduated from University with a Master's degree at age twenty one. I held top jobs and was always well paid and highly respected. I was an expert at relieving companies of large sums of money (in other words ripping off) and they couldn't prove that I did it. I had to do that to support my lavish lifestyle and when you are living lavishly you don't even remember how you came by the money, you just live as if it's your last day on earth. Whenever I was charged and taken to court I could afford the best lawyers money could buy and I also had people in top level positions in my back pocket. Well, the results were always the same, my lawyers were always able to twist the truth to my advantage then I would walk away a free, rich man. **But was I truly free from God's wrath?** Because after swearing on the Holy Bible and getting my way around man, then keeping large parties to celebrate victory and going back to live the same crooked way, I didn't care whose feelings I had hurt or what God they serve.

The case that got me here in prison was when I overstepped my boundary and brought pain and hardship on society, I interfered with what belonged to people who God looked out for most, the poor. Don't be fooled whenever anything is taken away from the people that need it most a curse will come upon you. People cried, fasted and prayed when their money disappeared and I believe that it was this desperate plea from the wilderness to God that brought about my ruins. This was the least amount of money that I had ever stolen from anyone and it brought me the harshest punishment, this time I could not celebrate. This money was donated by various organizations worldwide to feed, clothes and shelter people who didn't have anywhere to live and it was as if rats were eating at my conscience when I took their money. I respected only money and in so doing I always seen it as my god.

When I started reading the Holy Bible I saw these verses and if I had read the Holy Bible when I was free, I would not have done what I did. That's why I am making a plea to you to read the Holy Bible and trust and obey it. **(Proverbs Ch.10 vs. 2 states, Treasures of wickedness profit nothing: but righteousness delivers from death.) (1 Timothy Ch.6 vs.10 states, For the love of money is a root of all kinds of evil, and in their eagerness to be rich some have wandered away from the faith and pierced themselves with many pains.) (James Ch.5 vs.1-6) also gave a stern warning to the white collar criminal.**

Here in prison I am realizing that no money can replace my freedom and even though it is too late with man who has condemned me Christ Jesus will not but I must bare this punishment. My true freedom from the burden of guilt and shame is when I repented and ask Christ Jesus to forgive me. Only Christ Jesus can comfort and make me bare this punishment peacefully because on the real judgment day the truth cannot be twisted when you face God. ONE GOD!

<u>HIS POEM</u>

I WANTED TO BE MR. MAGNIFICENT

SO MY SINS WERE NO ACCIDENT

IT WAS LIKE HEAVEN SENT

WHEN I HAD SO MUCH MONEY TO SPEND

I KNEW BETTER BUT CHOSE TO BE DIFFERENT

SO WHAT I DID WAS MY OWN INTENT

IN HERE, EVEN WHEN MY PULSE BEAT IS EFFICIENT

ONLY CHRIST CAN MAKE ME CONTENT

FOR ME, I'VE LEARNT NOT TO WORRY ABOUT INCIDENTS

BECAUSE I'VE MADE THE BLOOD OF CHRIST SUFFICIENT

THE END

STORY 11

THE RACIST

ONCE THERE WAS a white man named Mr. Rocfool who was born and raised in South Africa during the wicked apartheid system. He had a wife who was born in the United States and a teenage son who was born in South Africa. When the apartheid system was discarded in South Africa where he lived in the nineteen nineties, Mr. Rocfool sold his property and packed all his belongings and migrated to the United States with his wife and son.

Mr. Rocfool bought property in a small town in North Carolina where the population in the town was less than fifty thousand, and about eighty miles from where his wife originated. This isolated property was ideally suited to Mr. Rocfool because coming from an apartheid system in South Africa he wasn't a people's person. He quickly settled into his new home but Mr. Rocfool had a serious problem, he was a sad racist, he didn't like anybody who was black and he made that known to all who lived in the vicinity of his home. Mr. Rocfool told blacks that he didn't want any of them on his property because they were cursed and the only time he would wear anything black would be his shoes where he can stand on it. He had a sign posted at the front of his premises saying the following words, **(Genesis Ch. 9 vs 25-27).** When you read in the Holy Bible the verses that were displayed on the sign, he says this is sure proof that the black man was cursed and no one should have any problem with his sign because these were the words of Noah in the Holy Bible that they have at home. Decent law-abiding citizens who saw the sign complained and reported it to the Sheriff but nothing could be done because the words were from the Holy Bible but his interpretation was not. A bishop from the community Church also tried to have a one on one conversation with Mr. Rocfool in regard to his interpretation of the scriptures but the bishop was rudely greeted by Mr. Rocfool cranking his shotgun and showing him his middle index finger and he had to back off.

In **(Genesis Chapter 9 vs 1)** we read where God Blessed Ham so how can drunken Noah overturn whom God had already blessed. No one in history had this type of power to override the great God almighty authority but this ignorance was still sadly preached by the white pastors in Churches in apartheid South Africa and made millions of black people lives miserable because of that apartheid practice. The pastor of the Church in the community would send several invitations to Mr. Rocfool but he would flatly refuse saying, "He does not want to mix with any black people who, though made free by the laws of man, are not his equal."

Every morning a young lad who is of Hispanic decent delivered Mr. Rocfool's newspaper to his house. One particular morning when the newspaper lad was making his delivery, Mr. Rocfool's German shepherd dog that had gotten used to the lad went out to collect the delivery. The dog was wagging his tail showing a gesture of friendship and the newspaper lad patted him on his head. Mr. Rocfool who was watching from his verandah shouted, "Why are you contaminating my dog, can't you read the sign at the front?" The newspaper lad answered, "Yes but I'm not black." Mr. Rocfool turned his water hose at the lad and aggressively shouted, "That's what you and your parents think, get off my property!" The newspaper lad rode off on his bicycle never to make another delivery at Mr. Rocfool's house again.

One day Mr. Rocfool's son Rex went hunting in the woods and his right leg accidentally got caught in one of the animal traps which Mr. Rockfool had set himself. The trap was so tight on his legs that Rex could not free himself so he had to wait several hours before a search party found him. The injury was very serious so Rex had to be rushed off to the hospital to get proper treatment because he had lost a lot of blood. While at the hospital the doctor told Mr. Rocfool that his son had a very rare blood type and that blood type which is found in one in fifty million people had to be found quickly or his son was going to die.

The medical lab staff went to work earnestly on the hospital computers checking medical records trying to find someone with Rex's blood type. After several hours of research the medical staff luckily located someone living about five hundred miles from the hospital in another state. Time was against them so they had to use a helicopter to cover the journey as quickly as possible. The pastor of the community Church accompanied the pilot to the destination.

While they were gone Mr. Rocfool and his wife waited at the hospital patiently with one of their white supremacy friends. But Mr. Rocfool had a serious issue with the hospital administration that caused him to verbally abuse the hospital staff using a number of expletives in the process. Mr. Rocfool's son Rex was sharing a hospital room with someone who was black and this upset him to the extent that he wanted Rex or the other patient to be removed because he claimed that he didn't want his son to be condemned like the black man. The hospital administration refused his request and Mr. Rocfool started a serious commotion in which security had to be called in to prevent him from disturbing other patients. Mr. Rocfool was confined to the waiting area by security and was told that the police would be called in if he continued with his boisterous behavior. He eventually calmed down after that stern warning and grumbled to himself in silence. They waited patiently and after about five hours waiting they heard the rattling of the helicopter landing on the hospital compound. Mr. Rocfool and his wife ran outside feeling very relieved until they saw who the blood donor was in the helicopter. It was an **Afro-American teenager** that they saw and this sent shockwaves in their brains causing Mr. Rocfool's blood pressure to skyrocket with him falling to the ground stuttering in a trauma-like situation. He was immediately stretchered off to emergency care and his wife who broke down in tears also accompanied him.

Without hesitation, the blood donor showing Christ like behavior was rushed to the emergency ward where Rex was. This is a clear situation that when you are washed with the blood of Christ Jesus you have to ignore all the wickedness that is done against you and show nothing but love, kindness and forgiveness. **The Holy Bible book of (Proverbs Ch. 25**

vs. 21-22) says, if your enemies are hungry give them food to eat and if they are thirsty give them water to drink; for you will heap coals of fire on their heads and Christ Jesus will reward you. Mr. Rocfool's friend who waited with him shook the pastor's hand and said thanks on their behalf. This was a clear indication that he was not as bad a racist as Mr. Rocfool. After about three hours the doctor came out smiling saying that everything was successful and Mrs. Rocfool could go in and see Rex. The blood donor was also okay but Mr. Rocfool remained in a state of shock for several days at the hospital before he could be released and taken home.

When Mr. Rocfool went home he felt so ashamed that he took down the sign at the front of his property and in an even bigger surprise he took up the pastor's invitation and went to Church, accompanied by his wife and son the following Sunday. Mr. Rocfool apologized openly to everyone in Church and told them that the love, kindness and forgiveness that were shown, Christ is definitely present there. He confessed to a silent Church with some members of the congregation being brought to tears listening to Mr. Rocfool's testimony that what they did was beyond the thinking of man because he would not have done the same if he was in their position. He also added that all the hate in his heart came from his ancestors who were taught by wolves in sheep clothing in the form of preachers who twisted the truth of the Holy Bible. The lies were so convincing that it had a devastating effect and caused millions to deviate from the one and true living God in Christ Jesus. Unfortunately, all the lies were passed down to generations. Mr. Rocfool said that his advice to future generations is that they must read the Holy Bible for themselves and reject anything that Christ did not stand for. Christ love is for all races and is everlasting. He said he was glad that while he was in the hospital bed he repented and asked Christ for forgiveness and he hopes everyone will forgive him for all the embarrassment he caused. "Thank you Christ Jesus!" he said. Mr. Rocfool started attending Church regularly and all warmly embraced him. Rex and the blood donor whose name is Dennis became good friends and communicated regularly through the electronic mail. ONE GOD!

POEM

GIVE GOD THE POWER

CAUSE ONLY HE KNOWS THE HOUR

SIN HAS NO COLOR

IT ONLY MAKES LIFE SOUR

LOVE SHOULD ALWAYS BE SHOWN TO ONE ANOTHER

NOT HATE OR TRYING TO BE A DESTROYER

IF YOUR NEIGHBOURS SHOULD BLUNDER

SHOW KINDNESS AND HELP THEM RECOVER

LET GOD'S WORD STAND LIKE A TOWER

BECAUSE BEFORE GOD, ALL ARE EQUAL AND NONE LOWER

THE END

STORY 12

ROMANCE NOVELS AND SOAP OPERAS

AFTER YEARS OF reading romance novels and watching soap operas on television one has to be very careful that what you read and see you don't get caught up into that lifestyle and put everything into practice. Most of what you read and see degrades, spoils and misleads married couples in regard to their families and God given duties that are set down in the Holy Bible. If you follow most of these romance novels and soap operas women are portrayed negatively and in view of that we have to remember that women are the sisters, aunts, daughters, cousins, wives and mothers of our nation. There is no me or you without a woman and even gays would agree to that because let's face it, no matter how some men might have a tough mind against women for whatever reason, their God given charm and beauty just cannot be ignored. In the Holy Bible one can just imagine how Adam felt when he was alone in the Garden of Eden before God created Eve as his companion.

Also children are most comfortable with their mothers in the early stages of their lives.

According to what we read in some romance novels and view on television in soap operas, we are going to look at the three types of women that they portray. The first one we're going to look at could be the worst of all three, she will have a wealthy husband who works his back off to make her feel like a queen and give her all the luxuries life can offer. With all of that she is willing to gamble the life of luxury which most women would die for and have a moment of indiscretion behind her husband back with someone who can't provide anything near to what she has. All this because she claims that her husband is always working, too tired, and has no time for her and cannot satisfy her sexual needs.

According to some romance novels and soap operas the second type of woman could be the greediest of all three. She will have a husband who is not rich, well rested and pays her all the attention in the world. Because of being well rested he makes love to her sometimes seven days for the week, twice on Sundays and still have enough energy to help her around the house. In spite of all his attention she still finds time to be unfaithful to him because she claims he cannot provide her with enough vanity to match up with the high profile friends she has.

The third woman is the most rare, not the most beautiful physically like the first two who most men are chasing but she is humble, has a loyal heart and very hard to find. She is the type the Holy Bible speaks about in the book of (Proverbs Ch. 31) as a virtuous woman and the kind of woman who is behind a successful man. She disciplines herself by reading her Holy Bible and obeys Christ Commandments. She keeps the ship steady with sometimes a minimum income and will never leave the ship even when the captain has gone overboard.

All three types of women in the stories have one thing in common they play hard to get at first even when they don't mean it. When the first two types of women are known in the stories, they end up being major heartbreakers and hard to please, hopping from bed to bed with different men and always using their beauty to lure men into a web of deception. I sometimes feel sorry for the men especially those without Christ in the stories because they always think they are strong and in charge but when the women display their powers the big strong loud mouth men are brought to their knees, signing any document, answering any questions and begging like babies. The women are always more dominant than the men in the stories and if you want to know how powerful a woman is or should I say how weak a man without Christ is, just check real life history and you will see how many men of great influence was brought to their knees by their powers. Instead of being leaders God want the men to be, they would fall victim to the woman's power which she won't hesitate to use when she wants her way. This indiscipline is one of the reasons why some women are getting so far ahead of some men today and try as you may if the man doesn't remember the teachings of Christ Jesus at all times it won't be easy to match her power. Great men in the Holy Bible have also fallen victim to the woman's power.

According to the Holy Bible we were all created in God's own likeness and image with a lot of emotion and jealousy. Read in Holy Bible (Exodus Ch.20 vs 5). Because of disobedience we have gone overboard with our interpretation of that chapter. Some romance novels and soap operas without knowing it have compared love to a green lizard that can change its color anytime or a switch that can be turned on or off with our fingers. The characters in the stories will only say or do what the other party wants to hear or see just to have their way and this is sad because the only time you will feel real emotional pain is when you love and get disappointed. Love according to the Holy Bible (1Corinthians Ch.13) is deep and is something that supposed to make us feel good at all times but because the end result makes us feel so bad and can cause so much pain in families, it is obvious that God did not create us to live that way. The romance novels and soap operas have wrapped a lot of evil things around love, for example, flirting, cheating, lying and when you think it couldn't get worse we see wives accidentally getting pregnant by their outside lovers and cannot afford their husbands to find out fearing divorce. The wives knew from the beginning that the outside lover only wanted to have a good time and no responsibility like what the husbands are burdened with at home but because things got so out of hand, they cleverly set up a gift wrap situation of the pregnancy then wickedly gives it to their husbands as a lifelong present. We have to be very careful we don't make that our way of life because we have situations in the stories where some wives have given many lifelong presents without their husbands ever finding out the truth and it's always the mothers in law who are first to suspect something is wrong. That type of life mocks the God of love in Christ Jesus who frowns on that type of living and He sees everything so why would we want to practice something which is painful to others and think we can get away with it.

Real life itself is a reflection of these romance novels in most cases but the part that disturbs me most is the fact that the women are blamed most of the times. I am not going to debate anything but I have seen in my life where some men had gotten good women in their lives and messed up big time all because of disobedience to the scriptures. So when Christ Jesus says in the Holy Bible those without sins cast the first stones in (John Ch.8 vs 7) we should remember and live by it and do to others as you would have them do to you (Matthew Ch.7 vs 12).

The ultimate sin that can arise out of any relationship and this is a serious warning to the men especially not to conduct themselves like the people in the stories. If you should turn up at home for some reason or the other unexpectedly and find your wife naked in bed with another man just like in the stories, please remember the words of Christ in the Holy Bible and do not be blinded by your emotions. Do not get into a fight with that man because she as much as him is a part of the act so she is equally guilty if he is not raping her. Too many times I've seen and heard on the news where the husband was blinded with jealousy and get into a fit of rage during the fight and killed her lover. When her lover is buried in the cemetery, the husband goes to prison for life because the horrible wife gave evidence in court against him. We all know after that terrible unfortunate situation sooner or later she is going to end up in another man's bed this time you can't do anything about it so it's always best to bite your lips turn and run fast. Remember that many fish are in the sea and wounds will heal so just keep going until you find another wife that will love and respect you or if you love her that much and she shows remorse the Holy Bible speaks about forgiveness as a practice for us. ONE GOD!

<u>POEM</u>

WHAT YOU DON'T SEE

WON'T TROUBLE YOU

WHAT YOU DON'T KNOW

WON'T BOTHER YOU

ONLY CHRIST LOVE

WON'T HURT YOU

IF ONE PERSON IS NOT ENOUGH

DO NOT SAY I DO

IF FRIENDS SPEAK UNGODLINESS

CHANGE THAT CREW

AND WHY DO SOMETHING

IF THERE'S A CHANCE OF FEELING BLUE

THE END

Printed in the United States
By Bookmasters